The Little Moose

Written by Ruth Martin ❄ Illustrated by Stephanie Boey

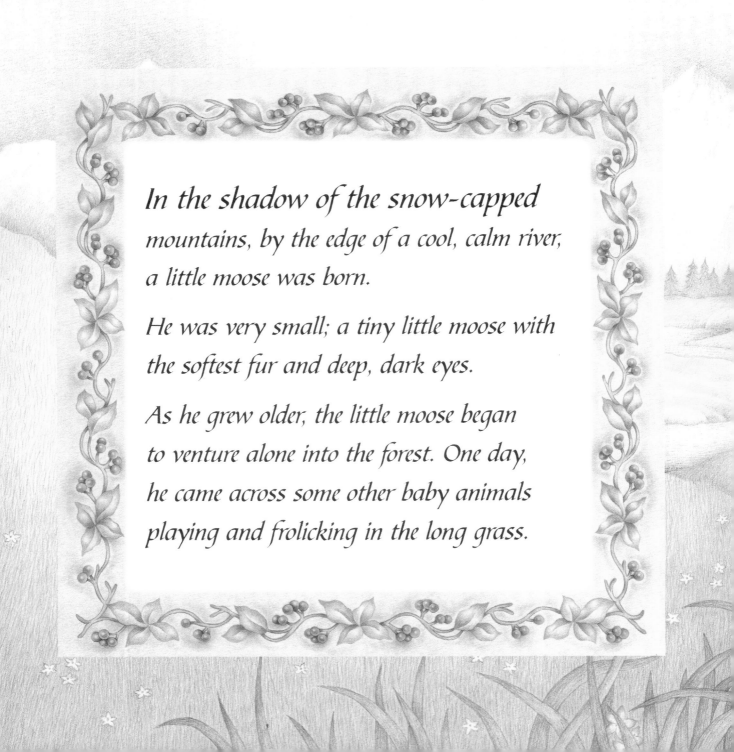

In the shadow of the snow-capped mountains, by the edge of a cool, calm river, a little moose was born.

He was very small; a tiny little moose with the softest fur and deep, dark eyes.

As he grew older, the little moose began to venture alone into the forest. One day, he came across some other baby animals playing and frolicking in the long grass.

The animals were playing a chasing game, laughing and singing,

"Eeny, meeny, miny, mo, catch a wolf cub by its toe, if it squeals, let it go. Eeny, meeny, miny MO!"

The little moose tried to ask if he could join in their fun, but in all the excitement, his little voice went unheard. He took a deep breath, steadied his legs, raised his head high and bellowed "HONK!"

The animals stopped their game and turned to look at him.

"Please may I play with you?" asked the little moose.

"You?" laughed the baby raccoon, his black and white tail quivering, "I've never seen such a small moose. You're not like the others — you're tiny!"

"Eeny Teeny Tiny Moose!" laughed the others in cruel delight, and they ran away, leaving the little moose very sad and all alone.

With his head hung in sorrow, the little moose returned home to his father.

"Dad…" he sighed. "I'm being called Teeny Tiny."

"That's OK, son," his wise dad told him.
"One day you will be King of the Forest, like me."

Teeny Tiny wanted to be a strong, mighty moose like his dad, so he stayed close, learning the ways of the forest and copying every move the elder moose made.

Together they loved to spend time rolling in the wallow, HONKING so loudly that the leaves shook on the trees.

When sometimes a rival moose appeared to challenge his father, Teeny stood safely back, watching the clash of huge antlers as his dad fought back bravely.

"My dad truly is the King of the Forest," thought Teeny Tiny proudly.

The two moose spent many happy seasons together, and soon Teeny was not so tiny. His favourite days were the ones they spent at the lake near the forest, dipping and diving in the clear water.

Late one autumn, as winter approached, Teeny and his dad were at the river, Teeny swimming stronger than ever, proudly waving his new-grown antlers above the water.

His father smiled, a little sadly, as he watched.

"Son," he said. "It is time for me to leave you. You must learn to journey alone, but we will find each other again. Go, now, and remember all I have taught you."

And before Teeny could protest or swim to the riverbank, his father was gone.

Teeny scrambled frantically to land, and saw the other animals gathered nearby, laughing.

"Look at you, Teeny!" they sneered, "All lost without your Daddy?"

Confused and upset, little Teeny ran from the others as fast as he could into the forest.

"*Honk!*" he called, hoping desperately to find his dad, but there was no sign. Finding a hollow tree trunk, Teeny curled up, exhausted and all alone. "What shall I do?" he wondered.

He slept awhile, and when he awoke the first winter snows were falling gently around him. He began to remember everything his father had taught him — that one day, he too could be King of the Forest — and it filled him with courage.

Setting out bravely into the forest, Teeny made his way towards home. He was alert to danger and it wasn't long before he heard a noise and his ears pricked up.

Crunch, crunch… "Grrrrrrr…"

Out of the trees ahead came a pack of wolves; hungry wolves – the terrors of the forest.

Antlers held high, Teeny ran towards the wolves, full pelt, bellowing as his father had taught him, so loudly that the leaves shook on the trees.

The wolves turned and fled.

Teeny ran and ran, enjoying his newfound strength,
until behind him he heard,

"Teeny! Stop!"

He turned to see the other forest creatures.

"We saw you scare the wolves! You're so brave!"

said the little raccoon. "Please will you be our friend?"

"Of course," said Teeny. "And will you help me find
my father?"

"I'm here," boomed the powerful voice of his father behind him.

"Well done, my boy. I am proud of you."

"I couldn't have done it without you, Dad!" sighed Teeny happily.

As the moon rose over the snow-capped mountains, everyone knew that soon there would be a new King of the Forest.

For my dear ole Dad — RM

For Shen Loong — SB

First published in Canada in 2008 by Fenn Publishing Company Ltd
34 Nixon Road, Bolton, Ontario, L7E 1W2, Canada.
Visit us on the World Wide Web at www.hbfenn.com

Devised and produced by The Templar Company plc,
The Granary, North Street, Dorking, Surrey, RH4 1DN, UK

Designed by Caroline Reeves

Edited by Stella Gurney

ISBN: 978-1-55168-332-4

CIP data available

Printed in Malaysia